To order additional copies of this book, contact:
Xlibris
844-714-8691
www.Xlibris.com
Orders@Xlibris.com

Illustrated by Rachael Plaquet

ISBN: Softcover   978-1-6698-3788-6
       EBook   978-1-6698-3787-9

Print information available on the last page

Rev. date: 07/13/2022

OH! THOSE CRAZY DOGS!

Tyse Comes to Visit

Dedicated to Amber

Introduction

This is a story about 2 crazy dogs, their adventures and the mischief they get into.

They are very loving dogs, but they can't help getting into things.

Hi ! I'm Colby! I'm big and red and furry ! I love everyone but sometimes people are afraid of me because I am so big!

Hi! I'm Teddy Bear! I'm big and white and very furry! I'm not as big as Colby, but just about. Everyone thinks I'm cute and I put shows on for them.

He puts shows on for everyone, rolls on his back and kicks his legs up.

Our owners picked us out specially and brought us home to love and care for us. We love them too, very much. They give us everything and a warm loving home. We will call them Mom and Pop.

Sometimes we don't listen to them, especially me, Teddi Bear!

but our Mom and Pop love us anyway. Sometimes I get Colby in trouble. I can get him to do anything I want because he loves me too and can't say no. He protects me all the time.

Tyse Comes to Visit

Mom and pop are happy today! Someone is coming to visit! Colby and Teddi Bear are watching mom and pop as they quickly tidy up and make some food. "Yum, yum" Colby and Teddi Bear say as they smell the food. "Let's go check the kitchen and see what they made" said Teddi Bear.

Colby and Teddi Bear quietly go into the kitchen and look at the food on the counters. "Oh wow!" exclaimed Teddi Bear. "What is all that?" "It sure smells better than our food!"

Teddi Bear asked Colby "Why don't you grab some of that for both of us?" Colby could easily grab the food because his head came right to the top of the counter. Colby looked at Teddi Bear and said "we'll get in trouble".

Teddi Bear said "so at least we will have eaten some really good food."

Colby looks at Teddi Bear and shakes his head. "O boy, the things I do for this guy!" Then he reaches up and grabs a mouthful of food and he and Teddy Bear run upstairs to the spare bedroom.

"They won't see us here" said Teddi Bear. They both ate the food, although they didn't know what it was called, it sure was good!

Not paying attention to the mess they made on the bedroom carpet Colby and Teddi Bear hurried downstairs because they heard someone come in the house. They both stopped at the bottom of the stairs. Mom was hugging someone she called Amber but there was a dog beside her. No one told us there was going to be another dog here.

Teddi Bear and Colby started barking at the dog as if they didn't know him. Mom turned around to look at us and frowned at our dirty faces. She didn't say anything because we had company! "Boys this is Tyse. He will be a real fun friend for you!" said mom.

Colby and Teddi Bear stayed where they were. Tyse slowly walked up to them with his tail wagging. "Hi" said Tyse. Colby and Teddi Bear looked at each other then at Tyse "Pretend we don't know you" said Colby. "Hi" they both said.

"Do you boys want to go outside to play?" asked mom. All three dogs ran to the patio doors and waited for mom to catch up.

Amber called Tyse and said "don't forget this!" Tyse turned around and ran to Amber, his mom, and grabbed a toy she held in her hands. It looked like something Tyse was good at playing with when they went to the circus. No one knew they had been together. Amber said "don't forget to share your balloon with Colby and Teddy Bear!"

Tyse ran out to the back yard where Colby and Teddy Bear were.

Teddi Bear saw Tyse with the balloon in his mouth and asked "how are you holding that?

Tyse said "I hold it by the nubby so I don't break the balloon!"

Both Colby and Teddi Bear asked at the same time "what is a nubby?"

Tyse laughed and said "It's where they tie the knot in the end of the balloon so the air doesn't get out."

"Oh!" said Colby and Teddi Bear. "What do you do with the balloon?" asked Colby. "Watch" said Tyse. And Tyse started jumping in the air and poking the balloon. Over and over he kept hitting the balloon with his nose as it came down. Sometimes the balloon would go way up in the air and Tyse would get it again.

Then he hit it over the pool. "That's mine!" said Teddi Bear and he jumped into the air to get the balloon over the pool. Well Teddi Bear got the balloon and splashed into the water with it, but he didn't get it by the nubby and BANG! The balloon broke in his mouth. "Wow" exclaimed Teddi Bear. "I'm so sorry I broke your balloon. I guess I didn't get it by the nubby!"

Tyse said "that's okay my mom will have some more. She always has them in her purse for me.

Tyse went to the patio doors and barked for his mom. Then all of a sudden someone yelled "who stained my carpet?"

"Oops run Colby!" Both Colby and Teddi bear ran but there really was nowhere to run to in the back yard. So they both jumped into the pool.

Tyse asked "can I come in too?' "Tyse loved to swim.

"Of course" replied Colby. "Come on!" Tyse ran down the stairs of the pool and started swimming toward Colby and Teddi Bear.

Amber called Tyse and said she had another balloon for him. When she saw the three dogs in the pool she laughed and walked over to Tyse. Amber threw the balloon at Tyse who hit it up high into the air.

Teddi Bear swam very fast to get the balloon where it was coming down. Teddi Bear got it! He hit it with his nose and Tyse got it again!

Then Tyse hit it toward Colby and he hit it back to Tyse. Amber was just staring at the three dogs who were playing pool balloon. She couldn't stop laughing as the three dogs kept treading water and hitting the balloon back and forth. Amber said "oh my gosh I have never seen anything like this before!

Tyse quietly said "she should have seen us at the circus! Colby and Teddi Bear laughed.

Soon mom and pop came out and forgot all about the stained carpet. "Oh my!" said mom. "this is almost like a circus!" They laughed and kept hitting the balloon back and forth between them in the pool and laughed again when mom commented about the circus. They didn't think mom and pop knew that they had met Tyse before.

Eventually the dogs got out of the pool and shook to get some of the water off. They lay down beside the pool in the sun to dry off.

Mom started watering her gardens which really interested Tyse. He slowly got up and walked toward mom. He was staring at the hose.

As mom was waving the hose around Tyse began jumping to catch the water. Mom said "Is there anything he doesn't do with water?"

"Not really, he loves water no matter where it comes from." replied Amber

Mom put down the hose and started deadheading the flowers. Tyse went over to the hose and started pawing at the nozzle which was sitting on it's lever. He pressed on the nozzle a couple of times and the water came out and sprayed him in the face.

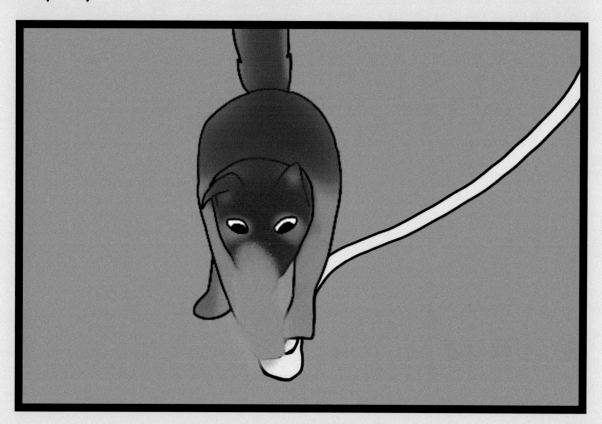

He shook his head and started pawing at the nozzle again and the water sprayed him in the face again. Everyone was laughing so hard they had to sit down.

He started pawing the nozzle again but it had turned sideways. He finally hit the handle and a full spray came out, but not at Tyse, it sprayed his mom, Amber! "Yikes" exclaimed Tyse, but everyone was laughing again. Amber joined in after a minute

"I can't believe how much fun these guys are having!" exclaimed mom who was standing at the patio doors. They're entertaining me too!"

Tyse looked around and saw pop stacking pieces of wood in the shed. Tyse ran over thinking to himself "I know where these go. I'm going to help him."

Tyse picked up a piece of wood and ran over to the fire pit at the back of the yard. He dropped it and ran back to the shed. Pop didn't see what Tyse was doing. Tyse kept picking up pieces of wood and dropping them by the firepit. He had a nice pile growing when pop suddenly turned around and saw all the wood by the fire pit.

"Oh no! I don't want the wood over there Tyse! Be a good boy and bring them back Tyse." Tyse just stood there looking at pop. He couldn't understand why pop didn't like what he had done to help him. So Tyse went to his pile of wood and grabbed a piece one at a time. He ran over to the side yard and put all the wood there.

Pop looked and said "No Tyse, not there, here. Everyone was looking at Tyse. He smiled and wagged his tail. He still thought he was helping pop.

"Hey Colby, Teddi Bear what do you want to do now?" he asked

"Hmm" Colby replied, "I think I'm going to rest in the shade here."

Teddi Bear said "Let's go for a swim in the pool!"

Okay "said Tyse "let's go!" Teddi Bear and Tyse ran as fast as they could to the pool and jumped as far as they could.

They both made a huge splash and got everyone wet.
Colby shook the water off himself and sprayed Amber
all over.

Teddi Bear and Tyse came out of the pool and they walked toward mom who was standing near a table on the patio. They both stopped and shook all the water out of their hair. "No" said mom.

She was soaking wet and so was all the food she had just put on the table. "Oh no!" said mom. "All the food is ruined!" "I'm sorry Amber but our meal is ruined!"

Amber said "that's okay my dog was responsible too. Let's see how we can fix this." As mom and Amber were carrying the dishes back into the house

Teddi Bear said" come on guys let's go and see if we can get any leftovers!"

"Oh no" said Colby "what is going to happen now?"

Tyse, Teddi Bear and Colby ran together toward the house and bumped right into the table with the remaining food on it. The food went flying all over the patio.

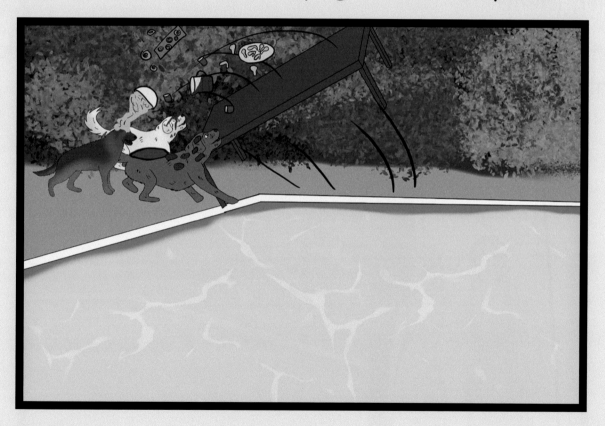

Colby, Teddi Bear and Tyse were covered in food. They started licking the food off each other. Pop came running from his wood pile, mom and Amber came out from the house to see the dogs covered in food and licking it off each other. "Oh my" said mom "what are we going to do with them?"

Amber shook her head and said "Tyse never behaves like this."

All of a sudden Colby ran to the garden. He saw a pretty butterfly and was trying to catch it. He was standing on his back legs and walking and his front paws were trying to catch the butterfly.

Mom told him not to catch the butterfly because he will hurt it if he does.

Colby said "I don't want to hurt it" so he got down on all feet and just watched where it was going while wagging his tail. It was so pretty and it kept going into mom's flowers. Colby watched it for a minute then walked back to Teddi Bear and Tyse.

Mom said "You boys stay right here. I have to hose you down to clean all the food off you. Mom and Amber cleaned all the dogs and toweled them down.

Teddi Bear yelled "lets go swimming!" and he ran and jumped back into the pool with a big smile on his face.

Mom and Amber yelled "no!" as Colby and Tyse followed. "Ahh so much for dry dogs!" exclaimed mom.

"I think I just need to sit here and relax, it's been quite a day. Not the kind of day I expected though."

"That's for sure" said Amber. So they sat and watched the three dogs chase each other in the pool.

Pop came outside and looked at the remaining mess and asked "What's going on?" While mom was explaining all that happened, the dogs saw pop and ran out of the pool to greet him.

"No, not again! said mom. And yes, all three dogs shook all the water out of their hair and sprayed everyone. Everyone was dripping wet. "Oh what can you do if you have a pool, expect to get wet!" said mom.

"I think the dogs are going in the house and they can stay in their beds for awhile. I've absolutely had it now. You guys get in your beds. Tyse you can lay on the rug between Colby and Teddi Bear." Mom's voice was mad so the dogs walked to their beds with their tails down between their legs.

They looked at each other and Colby said "I really do think we went too far today. We were just having so much fun we didn't think about what they would like. Which wasn't what they got."

"Really hard to tell them sorry." agreed Teddi Bear The dogs were sorry but they ended up falling asleep because they were so tired from they're activities.

Each of them was snoring, making a different sound and mom and pop laughed.

"Oh, those crazy dogs!

Thank you for choosing to read this book about the crazy dogs! I hope you enjoyed it and I hope you enjoy the next book about the crazy dogs and their winter adventure.

Books in the Oh! Those Crazy Dogs!
Series written by author CAL

Book 1   Colby Comes Home

Book 2   Teddi Bear Comes Home

Book 3   Teddi's First Time at the Cottage

Book 4   A New Friend in the Neighborhood! Digger!

Book 5   Colby and Teddi Bear Love Swimming in the Pool

Book 6   Colby and Teddi Bear Go to the Circus

Book 7   Tyse Comes to Visit

Book 8   Look for our next book coming soon!

Printed in the United States
by Baker & Taylor Publisher Services